engaged af!

soon to be mr. & mrs.

wedding date:

look at me
getting all
married & shit!

Wedding planner

WEDDING DATE & TIME:

TO DO LIST:

VENUE ADDRESS:

BUDGET:

OFFICIANT:

WEDDING PARTY:

NOTES & REMINDERS:

let's do this shit!

initial planning phase

IDEAS FOR THEME

IDEAS FOR VENUE

IDEAS FOR COLORS

IDEAS FOR MUSIC

IDEAS FOR RECEPTION

OTHER IDEAS

Notes & Ideas

Wedding budget planner

	TOTAL COST:	DEPOSIT:	REMAINDER:
WEDDING VENUE			
RECEPTION VENUE			
FLORIST			
OFFICIANT			
CATERER			
WEDDING CAKE			
BRIDAL ATTIRE			
GROOM ATTIRE			
BRIDAL JEWELRY			
BRIDESMAID ATTIRE			
GROOMSMEN ATTIRE			
HAIR & MAKE UP			
PHOTOGRAPHER			
VIDEOGRAPHER			
DJ SERVICE/ENTERTAINMENT			
INVITATIONS			
TRANSPORTATION			
WEDDING PARTY GIFTS			
RENTALS			
HONEYMOON			

this is going to get fucking expensive

wedding budget tracker

CATEGORY	BUDGET	ACTUAL COST	DEPOSIT	BALANCE

planning snapshot

CEREMONY EXPENSE TRACKER					
	BUDGET	COST	DEPOSIT	BALANCE	DUE DATE
OFFICIANT GRATUITY					
MARRIAGE LICENSE					
VENUE COST					
FLOWERS					
DECORATIONS					
OTHER					

NOTES & Reminders

NOTES & REMINDERS

RECEPTION EXPENSE TRACKER					
	BUDGET	COST	DEPOSIT	BALANCE	DUE DATE
VENUE FEE					
CATERING/FOOD					
BAR/BEVERAGES					
CAKE/CUTTING FEE					
DECORATIONS					
RENTALS/EXTRAS					
BARTENDER/STAFF					

NOTES & More

SPECIAL REMINDERS

planning snapshot

PAPER PRODUCTS EXPENSE TRACKER

	BUDGET	COST	DEPOSIT	BALANCE	DUE DATE
INVITATIONS/CARDS					
POSTAGE COSTS					
THANK YOU CARDS					
PLACE CARDS					
GUESTBOOK					
OTHER					

NOTES & Reminders

NOTES & REMINDERS

ENTERTAINMENT EXPENSE TRACKER

	BUDGET	COST	DEPOSIT	BALANCE	DUE DATE
BAND/DJ					
SOUND SYSTEM RENTAL					
VENUE/DANCE RENTAL					
GRATUITIES					
OTHER:					
OTHER:					
OTHER:					

NOTES & More

SPECIAL REMINDERS

planning snapshot

WEDDING PARTY ATTIRE EXPENSE TRACKER

	BUDGET	COST	DEPOSIT	BALANCE	DUE DATE
WEDDING DRESS					
TUX RENTALS					
BRIDESMAID DRESSES					
SHOES/HEELS					
VEIL/GARTER/OTHER					
ALTERATION COSTS					

NOTES & Reminders

NOTES & REMINDERS

TRANSPORTATION EXPENSE TRACKER

	BUDGET	COST	DEPOSIT	BALANCE	DUE DATE
LIMO RENTAL					
VALET PARKING					
VENUE TRANSPORTATION					
AIRPORT TRANSPORTATION					
OTHER:					
OTHER:					
OTHER:					

NOTES & More

SPECIAL REMINDERS

planning snapshot

FLORIST EXPENSE TRACKER

	BUDGET	COST	DEPOSIT	BALANCE	DUE DATE
BOUQUETS					
VENUE DECORATIONS					
BOUTONNIERES					
VASES/EXTRAS					
TABLE DECORATIONS					
OTHER:					

NOTES & Reminders

NOTES & REMINDERS

OTHER EXPENSE TRACKER

	BUDGET	COST	DEPOSIT	BALANCE	DUE DATE
PHOTOGRAPHER					
VIDEOGRAPHER					
CATERER					
HAIR/MAKEUP/SALON					
WEDDING RINGS					
WEDDING PARTY GIFTS					
OTHER:					

NOTES & More

SPECIAL REMINDERS

12 months before

SET THE DATE	CONSIDER FLORISTS
SET YOUR BUDGET	RESEARCH CATERERS
CHOOSE YOUR THEME	DECIDE ON OFFICIANT
ORGANIZE ENGAGEMENT PARTY	CREATE INITIAL GUEST LIST
RESEARCH VENUES	CHOOSE WEDDING PARTY
BOOK A WEDDING PLANNER	SHOP FOR WEDDING DRESS
RESEARCH PHOTOGRAPHERS	REGISTER WITH GIFT REGISTRY
RESEARCH VIDEOGRAPHERS	DISCUSS HONEYMOON IDEAS
RESEARCH DJ'S/ENTERTAINMENT	RESEARCH WEDDING RINGS

THINGS TO REMEMBER:

you fucking got this!

9 months before

- FINALIZE GUEST LIST
- ORDER INVITATIONS
- PLAN YOUR RECEPTION
- BOOK PHOTOGRAPHER
- BOOK VIDEOGRAPHER
- BOOK FLORIST
- BOOK DJ/ENTERTAINMENT
- BOOK CATERER
- CHOOSE WEDDING CAKE

- CHOOSE WEDDING GOWN
- ORDER BRIDESMAIDS DRESSES
- RESERVE TUXEDOS
- ARRANGE TRANSPORTATION
- BOOK WEDDING VENUE
- BOOK RECEPTION VENUE
- PLAN HONEYMOON
- BOOK OFFICIANT
- BOOK ROOMS FOR GUESTS

THINGS TO REMEMBER:

 6 months before

ORDER THANK YOU NOTES

REVIEW RECEPTION DETAILS

MAKE APPT FOR DRESS FITTING

CONFIRM BRIDEMAIDS DRESSES

GET MARRIAGE LICENSE

BOOK HAIR/MAKE UP STYLIST

CONFIRM MUSIC SELECTIONS

PLAN BRIDAL SHOWER

PLAN REHEARSAL

SHOP FOR WEDDING RINGS

THINGS TO REMEMBER:

3 months before

- MAIL OUT INVITATIONS
- MEET WITH OFFICIANT
- BUY GIFTS FOR WEDDING PARTY
- BOOK FINAL GOWN FITTING
- BUY WEDDING BANDS
- PLAN YOUR HAIR STYLE
- PURCHASE SHOES/HEELS
- CONFIRM PASSPORTS ARE VALID

- FINALIZE RECEPTION MENU
- PLAN REHEARSAL DINNER
- CONFIRM ALL BOOKINGS
- APPLY FOR MARRIAGE LICENSE
- CONFIRM MUSIC SELECTIONS
- DRAFT WEDDING VOWS
- CHOOSE YOUR MC
- ARRANGE AIRPORT TRANSFER

THINGS TO REMEMBER:

1 month before

- CONFIRM FINAL GUEST COUNT
- CONFIRM RECEPTION DETAILS
- ATTEND FINAL GOWN FITTING
- CONFIRM PHOTOGRAPHER
- WRAP WEDDING PARTY GIFTS
- CREATE PHOTOGRAPHY SHOT LIST

- REHEARSE WEDDING VOWS
- BOOK MANI-PEDI
- CONFIRM WITH FLORIST
- CONFIRM VIDEOGRAPHER
- PICK UP BRIDEMAIDS DRESSES
- CREATE WEDDING SCHEDULE

THINGS TO REMEMBER:

1 week before

- FINALIZE SEATING PLANS
- MAKE PAYMENTS TO VENDORS
- PACK FOR HONEYMOON
- CONFIRM HOTEL RESERVATIONS
- GIVE SCHEDULE TO PARTY

- DELIVER LICENSE TO OFFICIANT
- CONFIRM WITH BAKERY
- PICK UP WEDDING DRESS
- PICK UP TUXEDOS
- GIVE MUSIC LIST TO DJ

THINGS TO REMEMBER:

shit just got real!

1 day before

GET MANICURE/PEDICURE

ATTEND REHEARSAL DINNER

GET A GOOD NIGHT'S SLEEP!

GIVE GIFTS TO WEDDING PARTY

FINALIZE PACKING

TO DO LIST:

just fucking breathe

the big day!

GET HAIR & MAKE UP DONE

HAVE A HEALTHY BREAKFAST

ENJOY YOUR BIG DAY!

MEET WITH BRIDESMAIDS

GIVE RINGS TO BEST MAN

TO DO LIST:

this is it ! happy effing wedding day!

thoughts before the big day

Wedding planner

ENGAGEMENT PARTY:

DATE:

TIME:

LOCATION:

NUMBER OF GUESTS:

NOTES:

BRIDAL SHOWER:

DATE:

TIME:

LOCATION:

NUMBER OF GUESTS:

NOTES:

STAG & DOE PARTY:

DATE:

TIME:

LOCATION:

NUMBER OF GUESTS:

NOTES:

o.m.f.g.! this is really happening!

wedding party

MAID/MATRON OF HONOR:

PHONE: DRESS SIZE: SHOE SIZE:

EMAIL:

BRIDESMAID:

PHONE: DRESS SIZE: SHOE SIZE:

EMAIL:

BRIDESMAID #2:

PHONE: DRESS SIZE: SHOE SIZE:

EMAIL:

BRIDESMAID #3:

PHONE: DRESS SIZE: SHOE SIZE:

EMAIL:

BRIDESMAID #4:

PHONE: DRESS SIZE: SHOE SIZE:

EMAIL:

NOTES:

best fucking bride squad!

wedding party

BEST MAN:

PHONE: WAIST SIZE: SHOE SIZE:

NECK SIZE: SLEEVE SIZE: JACKET SIZE:

EMAIL:

GROOMSMEN #1:

PHONE: WAIST SIZE: SHOE SIZE:

NECK SIZE: SLEEVE SIZE: JACKET SIZE:

EMAIL:

GROOMSMEN #2:

PHONE: WAIST SIZE: SHOE SIZE:

NECK SIZE: SLEEVE SIZE: JACKET SIZE:

EMAIL:

GROOMSMEN #3:

PHONE: WAIST SIZE: SHOE SIZE:

NECK SIZE: SLEEVE SIZE: JACKET SIZE:

EMAIL:

GROOMSMEN #4:

PHONE: WAIST SIZE: SHOE SIZE:

NECK SIZE: SLEEVE SIZE: JACKET SIZE:

EMAIL:

hot af groom crew!

photographer

PHOTOGRAPHER:

PHONE: _____   COMPANY: _____

EMAIL: _____   ADDRESS: _____

WEDDING PACKAGE OVERVIEW:

EST PRICE: _____

INCLUSIONS:	YES ✓	NO ✓	COST:
ENGAGEMENT SHOOT:			
PHOTO ALBUMS:			
FRAMES:			
PROOFS INCLUDED:			
NEGATIVES INCLUDED:			

TOTAL COST:

Videographer

VIDEOGRAPHER:

PHONE: _____   COMPANY: _____

EMAIL: _____   ADDRESS: _____

WEDDING PACKAGE OVERVIEW:

EST PRICE: _____

INCLUSIONS: YES ✓   NO ✓   COST:

DUPLICATES/COPIES:

PHOTO MONTAGE:

MUSIC ADDED:

EDITING:

TOTAL COST:

NOTES:

dj/entertainment

DJ/LIVE BAND/ENTERTAINMENT:

PHONE: COMPANY:

EMAIL: ADDRESS:

START TIME: END TIME:

ENTERTAINMENT SERVICE OVERVIEW:

EST PRICE:

INCLUSIONS: YES   ✓   NO   ✓   COST:

SOUND EQUIPMENT:

LIGHTING:

SPECIAL EFFECTS:

GRATUITIES

TOTAL COST:

NOTES:

Florist

FLORIST:

PHONE: _____   COMPANY: _____

EMAIL: _____   ADDRESS: _____

FLORAL PACKAGE:

EST PRICE: _____

INCLUSIONS: YES ✓   NO ✓   COST:

BRIDAL BOUQUET:

THROW AWAY BOUQUET:

CORSAGES:

CEREMONY FLOWERS

CENTERPIECES

CAKE TOPPER

BOUTONNIERE

TOTAL COST:

wedding cake/baker

PHONE: COMPANY:

EMAIL: ADDRESS:

WEDDING CAKE PACKAGE:

COST: _____   FREE TASTING: _____   DELIVERY FEE: _____

FLAVOR:

FILLING:

SIZE:

SHAPE:

COLOR:

EXTRAS:

TOTAL COST:

NOTES:

transportation planner

TO CEREMONY: PICK UP TIME: PICK UP LOCATION:

BRIDE:

GROOM:

BRIDE'S PARENTS:

GROOM'S PARENTS:

BRIDESMAIDS:

GROOMSMEN:

NOTES:

TO RECEPTION: PICK UP TIME: PICK UP LOCATION:

BRIDE & GROOM:

BRIDE'S PARENTS:

GROOM'S PARENTS:

BRIDESMAIDS:

GROOMSMEN:

Wedding planner

BACHELORETTE PARTY:

DATE: _____ LOCATION: _____

TIME: _____ NUMBER OF GUESTS: _____

NOTES:

BACHELOR PARTY:

DATE: _____ LOCATION: _____

TIME: _____ NUMBER OF GUESTS: _____

NOTES:

CEREMONY REHEARSAL:

DATE: _____ LOCATION: _____

TIME: _____ NUMBER OF GUESTS: _____

NOTES:

Wedding planner

REHEARSAL DINNER:

DATE: _____

TIME: _____

LOCATION: _____

NUMBER OF GUESTS: _____

NOTES:

RECEPTION:

DATE: _____

TIME: _____

LOCATION: _____

NUMBER OF GUESTS: _____

NOTES:

REMINDERS:

names & addresses

CEREMONY:

PHONE: CONTACT NAME:

EMAIL: ADDRESS:

RECEPTION:

PHONE: CONTACT NAME:

EMAIL: ADDRESS:

OFFICIANT:

PHONE: CONTACT NAME:

EMAIL: ADDRESS:

WEDDING PLANNER:

PHONE: CONTACT NAME:

EMAIL: ADDRESS:

CATERER:

PHONE: CONTACT NAME:

EMAIL: ADDRESS:

FLORIST:

PHONE: CONTACT NAME:

EMAIL: ADDRESS:

names & addresses

BAKERY:

PHONE: CONTACT NAME:

EMAIL: ADDRESS:

BRIDAL SHOP:

PHONE: CONTACT NAME:

EMAIL: ADDRESS:

PHOTOGRAPHER:

PHONE: CONTACT NAME:

EMAIL: ADDRESS:

VIDEOGRAPHER:

PHONE: CONTACT NAME:

EMAIL: ADDRESS:

DJ/ENTERTAINMENT:

PHONE: CONTACT NAME:

EMAIL: ADDRESS:

HAIR/NAIL SALON:

PHONE: CONTACT NAME:

EMAIL: ADDRESS:

names & addresses

MAKE UP ARTIST:

PHONE: _____   CONTACT NAME: _____

EMAIL: _____   ADDRESS: _____

RENTALS:

PHONE: _____   CONTACT NAME: _____

EMAIL: _____   ADDRESS: _____

HONEYMOON RESORT/HOTEL:

PHONE: _____   CONTACT NAME: _____

EMAIL: _____   ADDRESS: _____

TRANSPORTATION SERVICE:

PHONE: _____   CONTACT NAME: _____

EMAIL: _____   ADDRESS: _____

NOTES:

caterer details

CONTACT INFORMATION:

PHONE: _____   CONTACT NAME: _____

EMAIL: _____   ADDRESS: _____

MENU CHOICE #1:

MENU CHOICE #2:

	YES ✓	NO ✓	COST:
BAR INCLUDED:			
CORKAGE FEE:			
HORS D'OEUVRES:			
TAXES INCLUDED:			
GRATUITIES INCLUDED:			

menu planner

HORS D'OEUVRES

1st COURSE:

2nd COURSE:

3rd COURSE:

4th COURSE:

DESSERT:

1 week before

	THINGS TO DO:	NOTES:
MONDAY		
TUESDAY		
WEDNESDAY		
THURSDAY		

REMINDERS & NOTES:

keep your shit together!

1 week before

	THINGS TO DO:	NOTES:
FRIDAY		
SATURDAY		
SUNDAY		

LEFT TO DO:

REMINDERS: NOTES:

so damn close!

Wedding guest list

NAME:	ADDRESS:	# IN PARTY:	RSVP: ✓

Wedding guest list

NAME:	ADDRESS:	# IN PARTY:	RSVP: ✓

Wedding guest list

NAME:	ADDRESS:	# IN PARTY:	RSVP: ✓

Wedding guest list

NAME:	ADDRESS:	# IN PARTY:	RSVP: ✓

Wedding guest list

NAME:	ADDRESS:	# IN PARTY:	RSVP: ✓

Wedding guest list

NAME:	ADDRESS:	# IN PARTY:	RSVP: ✓

Wedding guest list

NAME:	ADDRESS:	# IN PARTY:	RSVP: ✓

Wedding guest list

NAME:	ADDRESS:	# IN PARTY:	RSVP: ✓

Wedding guest list

NAME:	ADDRESS:	# IN PARTY:	RSVP: ✓

Wedding guest list

NAME:	ADDRESS:	# IN PARTY:	RSVP: ✓

Wedding guest list

NAME:	ADDRESS:	# IN PARTY:	RSVP: ✓

Wedding guest list

NAME:	ADDRESS:	# IN PARTY:	RSVP: ✓

Wedding guest list

NAME:	ADDRESS:	# IN PARTY:	RSVP: ✓

Wedding guest list

NAME:	ADDRESS:	# IN PARTY:	RSVP: ✓

Wedding guest list

NAME:	ADDRESS:	# IN PARTY:	RSVP: ✓

Wedding guest list

NAME:	ADDRESS:	# IN PARTY:	RSVP: ✓

Wedding guest list

NAME:	ADDRESS:	# IN PARTY:	RSVP: ✓

Wedding guest list

NAME:	ADDRESS:	# IN PARTY:	RSVP: ✓

Wedding guest list

NAME:	ADDRESS:	# IN PARTY:	RSVP: ✓

Wedding guest list

NAME:	ADDRESS:	# IN PARTY:	RSVP: ✓

Wedding guest list

NAME:	ADDRESS:	# IN PARTY:	RSVP: ✓

Wedding guest list

NAME:	ADDRESS:	# IN PARTY:	RSVP: ✓

Wedding guest list

NAME:	ADDRESS:	# IN PARTY:	RSVP: ✓

Wedding guest list

NAME:	ADDRESS:	# IN PARTY:	RSVP: ✓

seating chart planner

Table #

Table #

Table #

Table #

SEATING PLANNER NOTES:

seating chart planner

Table #

Table #

Table #

Table #

SEATING PLANNER NOTES:

seating chart planner

Table #

Table #

Table #

Table #

SEATING PLANNER NOTES:

seating chart planner

Table #

Table #

Table #

Table #

SEATING PLANNER NOTES:

seating chart planner

Table #

Table #

Table #

Table #

SEATING PLANNER NOTES:

seating chart planner

Table #

Table #

Table #

Table #

SEATING PLANNER NOTES:

seating chart planner

Table #

Table #

Table #

Table #

SEATING PLANNER NOTES:

seating chart planner

Table #

Table #

Table #

Table #

SEATING PLANNER NOTES:

seating chart planner

Table #

Table #

Table #

Table #

SEATING PLANNER NOTES:

seating chart planner

Table #

Table #

Table #

Table #

SEATING PLANNER NOTES:

seating chart planner

Table #

Table #

Table #

Table #

SEATING PLANNER NOTES:

seating chart planner

Table #

Table #

Table #

Table #

SEATING PLANNER NOTES:

seating chart planner

Table #

Table #

Table #

Table #

SEATING PLANNER NOTES:

seating chart planner

Table #

Table #

Table #

Table #

SEATING PLANNER NOTES:

seating chart planner

Table #

Table #

Table #

Table #

SEATING PLANNER NOTES:

seating chart planner

Table #

Table #

Table #

Table #

SEATING PLANNER NOTES:

seating chart planner

Table #

Table #

Table #

Table #

SEATING PLANNER NOTES:

seating chart planner

Table #

Table #

Table #

Table #

SEATING PLANNER NOTES:

seating chart planner

Table #

Table #

Table #

Table #

SEATING PLANNER NOTES:

seating chart planner

Table #

Table #

Table #

Table #

SEATING PLANNER NOTES:

seating chart planner

Table #

Table #

Table #

Table #

SEATING PLANNER NOTES:

seating chart planner

Table #

Table #

Table #

Table #

SEATING PLANNER NOTES:

seating chart planner

Table #

Table #

Table #

Table #

SEATING PLANNER NOTES:

seating chart planner

Table #

Table #

Table #

Table #

SEATING PLANNER NOTES:

seating chart planner

Table #

Table #

Table #

Table #

SEATING PLANNER NOTES:

seating chart planner

Table #

Table #

Table #

Table #

SEATING PLANNER NOTES:

Made in the USA
Monee, IL
19 September 2022

14289909R00063